Alice in Wonderland

WRITTEN BY MS. BOOKSY

STORY BY Clare Dill, Rachel Crouse, and Elizabeth Sussman
BASED ON Cool School created by Rob Kurtz
ART DIRECTION BY Dan Markowitz
ILLUSTRATIONS BY Giully Leão and Janice Rim

WIGGLE SNAP STORY TIME!

4

Once upon a time, a girl named Alice was walking in a park, when she saw something peculiar... a _white rabbit_ hopping by in a suit!

Oh dear, oh dear, I shall be late!

A rabbit in a suit? That can tell time?? And can talk???

Alice was very _curious_. Then she saw the rabbit jump down a rabbit hole.

Alice jumped down the rabbit hole too, and it was so colorful inside. It seemed *magical!* Instead of falling, she was floating down like a feather.

Alice landed in a strange room full of doors of many shapes and sizes.
On a table, there was a plate of delicious looking *cookies*.

Mmm... These cookies taste like pizza...
and ice cream... and pineapples!
I really like pineapples!

But suddenly, Alice started growing... and growing... and growing *so large* that her head touched the ceiling! She got scared that she was trapped, and started crying. Her teardrops were gigantic!

9

Eventually, she cried _SO_ much that her body completely ran out of tears, and she shrunk down. The puddles were large enough to swim in!

Luckily, Alice was a _really good swimmer!_
She started swimming and other animals joined her.

When Alice got to the shore, she met a *giant caterpillar!*
But Alice wasn't sure... Maybe the caterpillar was normal, and Alice was tiny?

Have you seen the White Rabbit?

Maybe... But you're not supposed to be here! I have to tell the Queen of Hearts!

Alice was scared, so she ran away from the caterpillar, and FAR away from any Queen of Hearts. Soon, she stumbled upon a _tea party_.

Ooh, a tea party?
A cup of tea will make
me feel better!

Alice sat down at the tea party and introduced herself.

Boy, were they *odd!* The March Hare would butter his toast, take a bite, and throw it away, again and again and again. #wasteful

The Mad Hatter was even _odder_. He kept dipping his pocket watch into a cup of tea! The clock was broken, and the hands were stuck at 4:00.

All of a sudden, a door opened in the tree behind Alice, and the *White Rabbit* hopped through.

Alice hopped through the tree, and popped out by an amusement park! But then she heard loud footsteps approaching.

Uh oh, I better hide!

It was the *Queen of Hearts*, marching with her army of playing cards!

The Queen put Alice on *trial*, with everyone else from Wonderland watching!

This was getting out of hand! Then Alice had an *idea*.

This is like a bad dream! But wait... If this is a dream, then all I have to do is...

It was a dream! Alice was back in the *park!* She must have dozed off, because the sun was setting. That meant it was almost dinner time.

Wonderland was a magical place, but Alice was excited to be home,
where things were as they should be. Although, for dinner,
Alice wanted pizza, ice cream, pineapple, and tea!

THE
END!

More Titles Available from Ms. Booksy!

For more Ms. Booksy, visit www.coolschool.com

Printed in Great Britain
by Amazon

18962867R00016